Sarah Emma Edmonds Was a Great Pretender

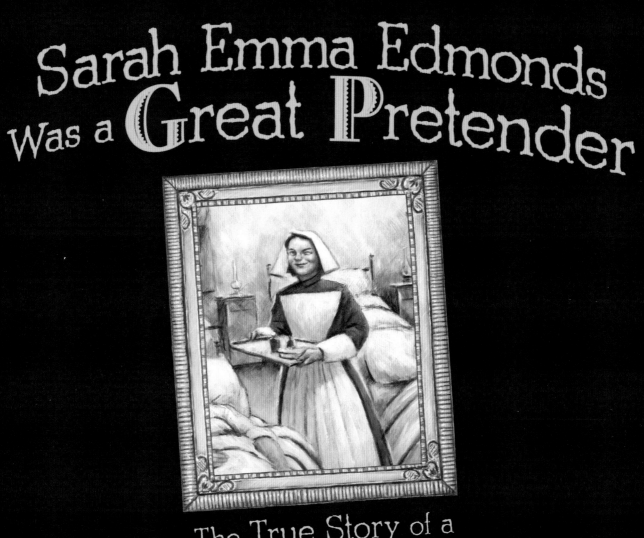

The True Story of a
CIVIL WAR SPY

Carolrhoda Books
A division of Lerner Publishing Group, Inc.
241 First Avenue North
Minneapolis, MN 55401 U.S.A.

Website address: www.lernerbooks.com

The image in this book is used with the permission of: Library and Archives Canada/Frank Thompson: her Civil War story/AMICUS 11061614/Page 20/nlc10241, p. 32.

Library of Congress Cataloging-in-Publication Data

Jones, Carrie.
    Sarah Emma Edmonds was a great pretender : the true story of a Civil War spy / by Carrie Jones ; illustrated by Mark Oldroyd.
      p.   cm.
    ISBN: 978–0–7613–5399–7 (lib. bdg. : alk. paper)
    1. Edmonds, S. Emma E. (Sarah Emma Evelyn), 1841–1898—Juvenile literature. 2. Women spies—United States—Biography—Juvenile literature. 3. Spies—United States—Biography—Juvenile literature. 4. United States—History—Civil War, 1861–1865—Secret service—Juvenile literature. 5. United States—History—Civil War, 1861–1865—Participation, Female—Juvenile literature. 6. United States—History—Civil War, 1861–1865—Women—Juvenile literature. 7. Nurses—United States—Biography—Juvenile literature. 8. Women soldiers—United States—Biography—Juvenile literature. 9. Impostors and imposture—United States—Biography—Juvenile literature. I. Oldroyd, Mark, ill. II. Title.
    E608.E235J66 2011
    973.7082—dc22
    [B]   2010028177

Manufactured in the United States of America
1 – DP – 12/31/10

To Rita Williams-Garcia
who retaught me the power
of pretending
—C.J.

To George and Jesse
—M.O.

Sarah Emma Edmonds Was a Great Pretender

The True Story of a CIVIL WAR SPY

Carrie Jones

ILLUSTRATIONS BY
Mark Oldroyd

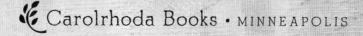
Carolrhoda Books · MINNEAPOLIS

Sarah Emma Edmonds is a girl.

She may look like a boy here, but she's only pretending. She started pretending really early.

Back in the 1840s in Canada, girls were not allowed to do many things. Sarah was very sad she wasn't a boy. Her father was too.

Sarah's father had a horrible temper. He treated Sarah badly. She thought if she were a boy he might like her. So Sarah spent a lot of her time trying to pretend she was a boy.

Sarah was always a great pretender.
That's what would make her a great spy.

(Although she wasn't a spy, at least not just yet.)

Eventually, she realized that her father would never be happy with a pretend boy. He'd always punish her for not being the real thing. So sometime in the 1850s, when she was a teenager, Sarah ran away to the United States.

She needed to make money to survive. (She couldn't pretend to eat.) She started selling Bibles door-to-door, traveling around the middle part of the country. It was unusual back then for a woman to travel by herself, and people weren't buying a lot of books. So, Sarah pretended to be a man. She bought men's clothes and cut her hair.

She called herself Frank Thompson. She started selling a lot more Bibles.

The Civil War began a few years after Sarah arrived in the United States. The war was fought between eleven Southern slave states (the Confederacy) and the rest of the United States (the Union).

The Confederacy wanted to leave the United States and form its own country.

In 1861, while she was waiting for a train, Sarah heard a newspaper boy on the street yelling that the president of the United States needed 75,000 men to fight for the Union. Sarah wondered,

"What can I do? What part am I to act in this great drama?"

Sarah hated the thought of not being involved in the war, of not helping. "Ten days after the president's proclamation was issued, I was ready to start for Washington," she wrote years later.

She enlisted in the Union army. At first, they rejected her—
rejected Frank Thompson, that is—because she was too small.

She tried again. She must have seemed bigger that time. She pretended her way through a bunch of questions and became a private and a nurse—a *male* nurse—in the Second Volunteers of the United States Army. They were sent south toward the fighting.

Being a nurse wasn't enough for Sarah, though. Her friend, James Vesey, had just been killed during a patrol. Sarah wanted to do more than heal her friends after they'd been hurt. She wanted to help prevent them from being hurt in the first place. A Union spy had recently been caught, and the Union needed someone else to spy. Sarah wanted the job.

Maybe spying just seemed natural to Sarah after so many years of pretending to be something she wasn't.

Sarah was still pretending to be Frank when she volunteered. So she was Frank when she was trained to be a spy. She studied maps and weapons and the personalities of the Southern commanders. She put silver nitrate on her skin to make it darker. She wore a wig. Not even the doctor she worked with as a nurse recognized her. Her pretending was working.

She took a new name—or, rather, Frank Thompson took a new name. This time she became an African American man, a slave.

Her new name was Cuff.

A chaplain's wife helped Sarah creep behind enemy lines. On the first day, Sarah helped other slaves build fortifications and ramparts. Her hands blistered, so she convinced another slave to swap jobs, and she worked in the kitchens. For three days, she counted guns, found out the plans of the Confederate army, and drew pictures of the Confederate defenses. She also learned all about the secret guns that weren't really guns at all. The Confederates had painted logs to look like giant cannons. It looked like Sarah wasn't the only one who knew how to pretend.

Once Sarah snuck back to her camp, she told the Union army everything she found out while she was pretending to be Cuff. She told them about the Confederate army and their plans and their pretend guns. The Union still lost the battle at Yorktown, but they didn't lose as many soldiers as they might have if Cuff—I mean Sarah—hadn't spied.

Two months later, she went back again.

This time she pretended to be Bridget
O'Shea, a chubby Irish peddler.
She was a woman (Sarah)
pretending to be a man (Frank)
pretending to be a woman (Bridget).

This would be confusing for most
people, but not for Sarah.

She sold items to the Confederate
soldiers and listened to try to find out
details about their war plans. When she
found out details, she would bring them
back to the Union army.

This time Frank's—I mean Sarah's—mission didn't go quite as smoothly. While dressed as Frank, she rushed off on a magnificent horse named Rebel. Rebel was cranky. (Maybe he knew Sarah was pretending.) He bit her arm when she dismounted to help a wounded soldier. Though terribly hurt, she eventually made it back to safety. Later, she stole another horse and rode through the battlefield to get back to the North.

When asked about how she managed to do all the pretending, Sarah once said,

"I am naturally fond of adventure, a little ambitious, and a good deal romantic—but patriotism was the true secret of my success."

Sarah went back to spy another time. This time she was an African American laundress. She colored her face again and talked with a huge accent. While cleaning clothes, she found official papers in the coat pocket of an officer. She took the papers and hid in the cellar of an old house just as a battle began. Bullets hit the house from all different directions. Somehow, huddled on the floor, Sarah survived. Perhaps she pretended that she was somewhere safe and warm where there was no war and no need for pretending.

All this time, the people she was spying for thought Sarah was a man. Frank Thompson was becoming a hero with a reputation for pluck, intelligence, and bravery. Then Frank—I mean Sarah—became sick with malaria, a deadly disease. Even though she was terribly sick, she couldn't go to an army hospital because then they'd discover she was a woman. Instead, she went to a private hospital in Illinois, planning to rejoin her unit as soon as she was well.

She never did. The army thought that her male identity, Private Frank Thompson, the amazing spy, had deserted. If she went back to the army as Frank Thompson, she would have been arrested. It was against the law to leave the army without permission.

So she stayed a woman and went back to working as a nurse—a female nurse. She pretended that she was never Frank Thompson, never a spy, never rode a horse named Rebel, and never stole Confederate secrets.

Sarah Emma Edmonds was a fantastic pretender.
No one had a clue.

AUTHOR'S NOTE

Some facts about Sarah Emma Edmonds are simple. She was born in northeastern Canada in 1841 and died in La Porte, Texas, in 1898. Between those years, she posed as a man and served with distinction in the Union army as a nurse and spy. Eventually, she told the truth and wrote her memoirs (all the quotes in this book are from her memoirs). To honor her devotion to her country, a group of Civil War veterans made her a member. She is the only woman to have such an honor, but certainly not the only one who deserved it.

Sarah Emma Edmonds as Frank Thompson
circa 1862

What's not so simple is *why* she did what she did. In the end, maybe we can only take her at her word: "I am naturally fond of adventure, a little ambitious, and a good deal romantic—but patriotism was the true secret of my success." In any case, she stands as but one example among many of a woman who made a great contribution to the welfare of her fellow humans in spite of the prevailing sexism of her era.

SELECTED BIBLIOGRAPHY

Edmonds, S. Emma E. *Nurse and Spy in the Union Army: Comprising the Adventures and Experiences of a Woman in Hospitals, Camps and Battle-Fields.* Hartford: W. S. Williams and Co., 1865.

Gansler. Laura Leedy. *The Mysterious Private Thompson: The Double Life of Sarah Emma Edmonds, Civil War Soldier.* New York: Free Press, 2005.

Reit, Seymour. *Behind Rebel Lines: The Incredible Story of Emma Edmonds, Civil War Spy.* Boston: Harcourt, 1988.

Seguin, Marilyn. *Where Duty Calls: The Story of Sarah Emma Edmonds, Soldier and Spy in the Union Army.* Boston: Branden Books, 1999.